WELCOME TO

RAVENS PASS

NO PLACE LIKE HOME

FINKELSTEIN
MEMORIAL LIBRARY
SPRING VALLEY, NY

by Steve Brezenoff
illustrated by Amerigo Pinelli

3 2191 00964 7602

Ravens Pass is published by Stone Arch Books
a Capstone imprint
1710 Roe Crest Drive
North Mankato, Minnesota 56003
www.capstonepub.com

Copyright © 2014 by Stone Arch Books. All rights reserved. No
part of this publication may be reproduced in whole or in part,
or stored in a retrieval system, or transmitted in any form or by
any means, electronic, mechanical, photocopying, recording, or
otherwise, without written permission of the publisher.

Cataloging-in-Publication Data is available at the Library of
Congress website.
ISBN: 978-1-4342-4615-8 (library binding)
ISBN: 978-1-4342-6215-8 (paperback)

Summary: The Mills family wants to leave Ravens Pass, but their
house has other plans…

Graphic Designer: Hilary Wacholz
Art Director: Kay Fraser

Photo credits:
iStockphoto: chromatika (sign, back cover); spxChrome (torn
paper, pp. 7, 15, 25, 29, 39, 51, 63, 73, 85)
Shutterstock: Milos Luzanin (newspaper, pp. 92, 93, 94, 95,
96); Robyn Mackenzie (torn ad, pp. 1, 2, 96); Tischenko Irina
(sign, pp. 1, 2).

Printed in the United States of America
in Stevens Point, Wisconsin.
082013   007666R

Between where you live and where you've been, there is a town. It lies along the highway, and off the beaten path. It's in the middle of a forest, and in the middle of a desert. It's on the shore of a lake, and along a raging river. It's surrounded by mountains, and on the edge of a deadly cliff. If you're looking for it, you'll never find it, but if you're lost, it'll appear on your path.

The town is **RAVENS PASS,** and you might never leave.

TABLE OF CONTENTS

Chapter 1
A FRESH START

Ravens Pass was covered with snow. The houses on Juniper Street looked like models in a holiday-themed railroad set.

As the early night fell over the town, the streetlights came on, and lights came on inside the houses. Ravens Pass — especially that block on Juniper Street — looked like the most perfect place in the world.

But the snow covered the ugly truth. Ravens Pass was the center of all things evil.

In fact, the town was a haven for creatures of the night, for users of dark magic, and for all the monsters you ever had nightmares about.

Theresa and Jay Mills didn't know that, though. Not really. All the kids in Ravens Pass suspected their town was kind of creepy, but they didn't quite know why.

That evening, they were on their front lawn, heaving snowballs at each other. "I can't wait to get out of this place," Jay said. He was in seventh grade at Ravens Pass Middle School. This was his winter break, though, and he sure wasn't thinking about school.

Jay tossed a snowball across the lawn. It missed his little sister by a few feet.

"Ha," Theresa said. "Nice try." She packed a snowball of her own.

Before she could launch the snowball, her brother tackled her. They both tumbled into the fresh snow.

"It's down my neck!" Theresa shouted. "Get off me!"

Jay laughed. "Don't worry," he said. "We'll be living down south soon. Then there won't be any snow for me to torture you with."

Just then, the front door swung open. Its hinges squeaked, and the ragged screen door slapped against the front of the house. It was an old house, so something always needed fixing.

Mom rolled her eyes. "Fighting again?" she said. "You two come inside and get cleaned up. The pizza will be here soon."

"Yeah!" said Jay. "More pizza!"

Jay climbed off his sister and brushed the snow off the front of his coat.

Theresa sat up in the snow. "I'll eat Ravens Pass Pizza every day between now and when we leave," she said. "It's the best pizza in the world."

Jay nodded. "True," he said. "That is one thing I'll miss about this place."

Just then, a little hatchback with a bright red sign on the roof pulled into the driveway. The pizza delivery driver climbed out. He was a big man with a white beard. In his red uniform, in the snow-covered yard, he looked like another famous deliveryman.

"Hey, hey!" the driver said as he walked around the car to grab their pizza from the passenger's seat.

"Hi, Davey," Theresa said.

Jay walked with the driver toward the house. "Theresa and I were just saying how much we'll miss Ravens Pass Pizza," he said.

"Miss it?" Davey asked. "Why would you stop eating it in the first place?"

"We're moving," said Theresa. "Dad got a new job."

"Down in Florida," said Jay, smiling. "I'm going to learn to surf as soon as we get there."

Davey whistled. "Sounds pretty cool," he said. "But I could never leave Ravens Pass."

Jay gave him a sour look. "You mean you actually like it here?" he asked.

The door opened. "Would you two come inside already?" Mom said. Then she saw Davey. She took the pizza and paid him for it.

When she was back inside, Davey turned to Theresa and Jay. "I didn't say I like it here," he whispered. "I said I could never leave."

Then he walked back to the car, got inside, and drove away.

Chapter 2

WON'T BUDGE

Over the next few days, the inside of the Mills' house looked less and less like a home, and more and more like a warehouse for cardboard boxes. All the books were in boxes. All the pictures were in boxes. There was even a box filled with canned goods and old bottles of spices and herbs.

On Saturday morning, Dad picked up the rental truck. It was parked outside.

"Wake up, Jay!" his mom called through his bedroom door. "Time to finish packing."

He rolled over and found his glasses so he could see the clock. It was only six a.m. "It's too early," he called back.

But Mom had already gone down the hall to wake up his sister. Jay rolled out of bed, put on his slippers, and headed down for breakfast. "I can't pack on an empty stomach," he mumbled to himself.

"Me neither," said Theresa, joining him on the stairs.

When they reached the kitchen, they found a box of cereal and a carton of milk on the table. It was the only food left in the house. Mom and Dad were arguing in the living room.

"Darling," Dad said, "I hung the thing myself. It's just hanging on a nail."

"Oh?" said Mom. "Then why won't it budge?"

Theresa and Jay exchanged a glance. They went into the living room to investigate.

Mom was standing on a chair with her hands on her hips. Next to her, on the wall, hung a small clock. Dad was standing next to the chair, sipping his orange juice.

"This is ridiculous," Dad said. "Please get down from there and I'll take it off."

Mom sighed and got down from the chair. "Be my guest, smarty-pants," she said.

Dad cleared his throat and handed Mom his glass of juice. Then he climbed onto the chair and grabbed the clock with one hand. He gave it a little tug, but it didn't budge.

"The nail must be snagged on something," he said.

Dad pressed his face against the wall, trying to get a look behind the clock. "I can't really see anything back there," he said.

He tugged again, and the clock slammed against the wall. It wouldn't budge again. "I swear, it's like it's holding on for dear life," Dad said.

He glanced down and saw Jay looking up at him. "Go to the garage, Jay," Dad said, "and get me my crowbar."

Jay sighed. He headed through the kitchen, and then out the door. It was cold in the garage, so his slippers weren't much defense against the chilly cement floor.

The garage was full of boxes, just like the house was, but these boxes had been there for as long as Jay could remember. Most of them were bent, torn, and wet.

Jay poked around in the boxes, looking for a big, metal crowbar. Instead, he found old, grimy junk. There were old seed packets, rusty screwdrivers, garden tools, and half-empty bottles of motor oil. But no crowbar.

In one box, he found a dust-covered, framed needlepoint. He pulled it out. It looked old — older than his parents. Older than his grandparents, even. In fact, it looked like maybe his grandmother's grandmother might have made it.

The needlepoint had gold lettering on a blue field. There were trees in the center of the picture. The sun was in one corner, and the moon in the other corner. At the bottom, right in the middle, was a house. It looked just like his house.

Across the center, in gold lettering, it read, "There's No Place Like Home."

"Jay!" called his dad from inside the house. "What's the holdup?"

Jay put down the framed needlepoint. "I can't find it!" he shouted.

"It's hanging behind the door!" Dad called back.

Sure enough, there it was. Jay grabbed it and hurried back inside, shivering as he went.

Jay handed the crowbar to his dad. "Here," he said.

Dad forced the end of the crowbar under the top of the clock. Then, with a grunt, he pried as hard as he could. The clock put up a good fight, but it finally sprang off the wall, taking a big chunk of plaster and paint along with it.

Mom jumped back. "My goodness!" she shouted. Dad nearly fell off the chair.

Theresa ran to the far wall where the clock had slammed against the floor. She picked it up. A piece of the wall was still stuck to its back. "Wow," she said.

As Dad climbed down from the chair, the floor and walls in the living room creaked and sagged. And a strange moaning sound filled the room.

"Weird," Dad mumbled.

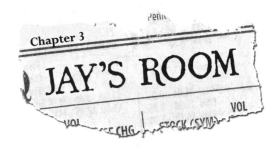

Chapter 3
JAY'S ROOM

Jay headed upstairs to pack up the rest of his room. "This shouldn't be too hard," he said to himself.

His plan was to simply stuff everything into cardboard boxes. He wasn't concerned with anything being in the right place, since nothing was in the right place in his room anyway. He pulled his desk chair up to his bureau, planted a fresh cardboard box on it, and began dumping the contents of the bureau into the box.

"This is easy," he said, smiling. "I don't understand why it took Mom and Dad so long to pack their stuff."

Jay knocked action figures off shelves and right into the box. He tossed a pile of shirts — clean and dirty ones — in on top of them. He dropped three pairs of sneakers in next. Then he got down on all fours to check under the bed. As he did, he heard a door creak behind him.

"Hello?" he said with his head still under the bed. No one answered, so he shimmied out from underneath. His bedroom door was closed, but his closet door was open — just a little.

"Is that you, Theresa?" Jay said. He took a step toward the closet, and the door slammed shut.

Jay tugged on the door. It wouldn't budge. "You better open this door, Theresa," he said.

Theresa didn't reply, but the door still wouldn't budge. "Open this door right now," Jay said, "or I'll tell Mom and Dad that you're not packing."

He gave the doorknob one more big tug. This time the door flung open easily, sending Jay sprawling backward. "Ow," he said, rubbing the spot on his shoulder where he hit the floor.

Jay stared at the closet. He expected to see Theresa standing there, giggling or crying or something. But there was no one there!

Unless, of course, Theresa was hiding behind Jay's old clothes in the back of the closet. Jay smiled and dove into the closet.

As he reached the back, thinking he'd find his mischievous sister, the closet door swung closed, then locked.

He was trapped in darkness.

Chapter 4

THERESA'S ROOM

Down the hall in her room, Theresa was packing up her belongings. She had a box for each category of item, including one box for her little ceramic figures of elves, dragons, unicorns, and wizards.

The first figure she had ever gotten was a gift on her eighth birthday. Now, at age eleven, she had quite a collection.

Carefully, she wrapped each piece in tissue. Then, she wrapped each piece again in a T-shirt.

Finally, Theresa put each little bundle into the box marked "Collection." It was boring work, but it was important. Each of the little statues meant a lot to her.

Theresa picked up a statue of a wood fairy. This one was painted green, pink, and blue. It had little, plastic, shiny gems for eyes. It was one of her favorites.

Then she heard the moaning again. It sounded just like the moaning she heard when Dad had ripped the clock from the wall.

She carefully set the fairy down and went to the door. "Hey, guys! Is everything okay down there?" she called downstairs.

The only reply was more moaning. "What is that noise?" she called out. No one answered. "Mom? Dad? Jay?"

Theresa stood in the open doorway a moment, waiting for a response. But there was only silence. The moaning had also stopped.

Theresa shrugged.

She returned to her statues to finish preparing them for the move. The moment she picked up the wood fairy, though, she heard the moaning again. But this time it was coming from somewhere inside her room.

Theresa backed up against her bureau. The remaining statues on top of it teetered back and forth, but didn't fall. "Who's there?" she said. "Jay, this isn't funny."

But there was no answer. Only some more moaning.

It's coming from the floor! Theresa realized.

Theresa noticed a dark spot on the carpet. "It's coming from that corner," she said.

She took a step toward the spot, and the moaning grew louder. It was like a deep, sorrowful cry. Theresa imagined it was the sound a unicorn would make if it was hurt or dying.

She lowered herself to the ground and crawled to the corner. Immediately, the moaning grew even louder.

"What is that noise?" Theresa said. She pressed her ear to the thick carpeting. "It's definitely coming from right here."

The moaning shook the floor. Whatever was making this sound, it was in trouble, and Theresa had to help it.

Theresa stared at the corner of the carpet.

The very edge of the carpet was pulling up from the floor a little. She could easily yank it up to see what was underneath.

But if she did, her mom would throw a fit.

"We're leaving this old house soon, anyway," Theresa whispered. As if in response, the moaning grew even louder. It sounded so scared, and desperate.

Theresa couldn't resist any longer. She grabbed the corner of the carpet. With all her strength, she tugged it from the floor.

Under the carpet was a thin layer of foam. She quickly pulled that up too, revealing a large section of the original hardwood floors that were underneath.

The moaning suddenly stopped.

Before her eyes, the wood floor began to change colors. Not all over, but just in a few spots. It looked like an invisible finger dipped in black ink was moving slowly across the wood.

Theresa jumped to her feet and stared down at the growing streaks of black. Then the smell of burning wood was filling the room.

"Dad!" Theresa shrieked, but she didn't move. She just stood there, staring down at the floor. Soon, the streaks took shape. They formed letters.

EAVE.

"Eave?" Theresa said. "What does that even mean?"

Theresa caught the scent of something strange. She turned around to see burning fragments of carpet and foam.

The smoldering pieces were creating thick, acrid smoke. The billows of smoke were quickly filling her room.

"What is going on?!" Theresa cried. She called out for her parents, then remembered that they hadn't responded to her calls earlier.

Theresa realized she was on her own.

She grabbed the pulled-up corner of the carpet and ran to the far corner of her room with it, pulling up as much of the burning carpet and foam as quickly as she could.

With that done, she pushed the carpet aside to clear the area. Then she turned to face the smoke-filled room.

Coughing, she got down on her knees and crawled along the floor toward where the writing was.

Now Theresa could read the whole message.

YOU CAN NEVER LEAVE.

Theresa screamed. She threw open the door and ran downstairs.

Chapter 5

IRON CLAWS

"I just can't imagine what you were thinking," Mom said as she paced in front of the couch where Theresa and Jay sat.

Dad sat in his recliner, leaning forward. His head was in his hands. "Have you both gone insane?" he muttered.

"Jay, first I find you locked in your own bedroom closet," Mom added. "And Theresa . . ." Mom stopped pacing and stared at her daughter. "The Theresa I know would never tear apart her own room."

"It's not like you at all," Dad added.

Theresa kept her mouth shut. She'd tried denying it over and over, but it was no use.

Jay had done the same. He'd sworn up and down that he hadn't locked the closet door on himself. He'd even tried blaming Theresa, but that had only made it worse.

Dad leaned closer from his chair. "If we didn't have so much packing left to do," he said, "I'd ground you both for the rest of the month."

"But that's not an option," Mom said. "Now come into the dining room. We need your help moving the table and chairs into the back of the rental truck."

Muttering to themselves, Theresa and Jay followed their parents into the dining room.

The dining room was mostly empty now. Only the tables and chairs remained. They were big, old, and made of heavy wood, and they'd been in the family for generations. They'd probably been in this house for generations.

Jay wrapped his hands around the seat of one chair and tried to pick it up. "Ugh!" he said with a grunt. "Are these things made of stone?"

He let go, rubbed his hands together, and caught his breath.

Dad scratched his head. "I thought the same thing," he said.

"Nonsense," said Mom. "We move these chairs all the time." She walked over to a chair and pushed it across the floor a few feet toward the kitchen. "See?"

"Try to pick it up," Jay said. "I bet you can't."

He was wrong. She had no problem picking it up and putting it right back down.

Jay tapped his chin, deep in thought.

"What is it?" Theresa whispered in his ear.

Jay shook his head. "Mom," he said. "Try to bring it out to the truck."

Mom shrugged. She casually reached for the chair and tried to pick it up. It didn't move.

"Problem?" Dad said, snickering.

"I can't lift it!" Mom said.

Theresa squinted at Jay. "How did you know?" she whispered.

"Let's all try," Dad said. Jay winked at Theresa, and the two of them joined Mom and Dad.

It took all four of them, lifting with all their combined strength, to get the first chair out to the truck.

Afterward, everyone was exhausted. Theresa and Jay each grabbed a lemonade from the cooler in the kitchen.

"This is nuts," said Mom. She sat down in the front hall and took a sip of her iced tea.

Dad tossed the screwdriver into the air, and then caught it. "Let's get the rest of the dining room loaded later," he said. "I'll start on the curtain rods for now."

"Oh, leave the curtain rods," Mom said.

"Nonsense," said Dad. "These curtain rods were handmade by my great-grandfather. I'm taking them with us."

Theresa and Jay went into the living room with their lemonades. They watched Dad unscrew the bolts that held the rod above the window.

The curtain rods were made of heavy, dark iron. The middle of the rods were twisted and curled in tiny, complicated patterns. At each end was an iron claw that looked like the talon of a great bird of prey.

"They are pretty cool," Theresa said. "They're like dragon curtain rods."

"The last screw," said Dad, holding it in place. "Jay, come and grab this —"

Suddenly, the claws clicked and clacked to life. They reached out from the wall. One iron claw grabbed hold of Dad's arm, and the other went for his throat.

"Dad!" Theresa shouted. Jay dashed forward and tried to pull his father away from the rods.

"Mom, help!" Theresa shrieked, running into the front hall.

Mom dropped her glass and ran into the living room just as Dad fell from the stepladder. He fell right into Jay and Mom's arms. The curtain rod, now stiff as iron and back to its normal shape, fell to the wood floor with a loud clank.

"What happened in here?" Mom asked.

Dad got to his feet and dusted himself off. "The curtain rod," he said, out of breath. "It — it came to life!"

Jay and Theresa nodded wildly.

Mom rolled her eyes at Dad. "Came to life," she said. "Right, right."

"And attacked me!" Dad said. "Okay, I know it sounds crazy —"

"It is crazy," Mom said. "Iron curtain rods don't come to life."

"Sorry," Dad said. "I'm sure you're right. I'm just really tired. And twice as stressed."

Mom put her arm around him. "We all are," she said. "Between moving and starting new jobs and new schools in a new state. That's a lot."

Dad nodded. He looked exhausted.

"Come on," Mom said. "I'll make you a cup of tea." She led him into the dining room.

Jay and Theresa watched them go. "Something funny is going on," Jay said.

"That's the understatement of the century," Theresa said. "A curtain rod just tried to kill Dad!"

Jay was deep in thought. Theresa watched him a moment. Then she said, "Hey, how did you know?"

"Huh?" Jay said. "Know what?"

"About the chair," Theresa said. "It seemed like you knew Mom wouldn't be able to move it when you suggested she should try to take it to the truck."

"I think it's the house," Jay said. "I think the house won't let us move out."

Theresa's eyes went wide. "The floor," she said. "It said we'd never leave!"

Jay nodded. "And my closet tried to lock me inside," he said.

"So what do we do?" Theresa said. "Google 'haunted houses,' or something?"

"We can't," said Jay. "Everything is packed, and the Internet and cable are turned off already."

Theresa thought for a moment. She smiled. "Then let's go to the library."

Chapter 6

A SPELL

Mom and Dad weren't thrilled about Jay and Theresa taking off in the middle of packing. Neither did they like the idea of the two of them biking to the library in the snow. But everyone was exhausted and stressed and needed a break. So their parents let them go.

The roads were slushy Theresa and Jay pedaled carefully and slowly along the deserted winter streets of Ravens Pass. It was slow going, but manageable.

Soft, yellow lights shined from the big front windows of the Ravens Pass Library.

As they chained up their bikes, Theresa and Jay could see the librarian at her big desk near the door.

Inside, it was warm and quiet, quieter than it had been outside. Here, there wasn't the sound of winter wind and their bike tires spinning in slush.

Theresa sat down at the computer closest to the door. Jay pulled up a chair and joined her.

"Try searching for 'haunted house,'" Jay suggested. Theresa typed it in. A bunch of old horror movies popped up. None of them looked very good.

"How about 'spells for houses'?" said Theresa. She tried that too.

Theresa found a list of spells to protect a house, to make a house happy, and to keep a house safe. But there was nothing about keeping a family in a house against their wishes.

After an hour of more searches and zero results, Jay slumped back in his chair. "I'm out of ideas," he said.

"We better get home," Theresa said, starting to stand up.

"You kids are looking in the wrong place," said a voice behind them.

Both Jay and Theresa spun around. The old janitor, a man who seemed about a hundred years old, stood there with his big broom. He was covered head to toe with green clothes.

"What do you mean, Mr. Jenkins?" Jay asked.

"I was listening to you," he said, leaning over. His skin was wrinkled and dry, like slept-in clothes. "I heard what your problem is. And I know where you should be looking for the answer."

"It's rude to eavesdrop," said Theresa, crossing her arms.

"If he can help us," Jay said, "then it's okay."

Mr. Jenkins grinned. He rested his elbow on his upright broom handle. "Smart boy," he said. "Come with me."

Mr. Jenkins led them to the stairwell. They followed him down three stories.

"I didn't know the library went this deep," Theresa said quietly.

"There's a lot you don't know about this town," said Mr. Jenkins.

"And most of it," Mr. Jenkins said, "you don't want to know. Believe me on that."

Jay glanced at Theresa. She grabbed his hand.

The stairwell grew darker as they reached the door at the bottom.

Mr. Jenkins pulled a key ring from his belt. He selected one particular key, then opened the door with it.

"This is where you need to start your search," Mr. Jenkins said. He stepped into the dark, musty room. There was a bright flash as the janitor lit an old gas lamp along the wall. A gentle, flickering light filled the room.

Now the kids could see the room was filled with books. Not ordinary books like they had upstairs, though. These books were covered in dust and spiderwebs.

All of the books were bound in dark brown or black leather.

"Over here," said Mr. Jenkins.

He stood in the very middle of the room at an old reading desk. He'd taken a book from the shelves and opened to a page near the front. "This book contains the history of Ravens Pass," he said.

Mr. Jenkins laughed. "Well," he added, "its *special* history."

"What do you mean?" asked Theresa. She stood next to him and tried to get a look at the book. The writing didn't make any sense to her. She recognized the letters, and even some of the words, but when she tried to read them the letters seemed to swim around the page.

Jay looked over Mr. Jenkins's shoulder. "It's all nonsense," said Jay.

"To you, maybe," said the old janitor. "But to those who understand, it is great wisdom."

Mr. Jenkins tapped a wrinkled and bent finger on the page. "Here," he said, "is a drawing of your neighborhood."

Jay and Theresa squinted at the page.

What had been a jumble of lines slowly began to take form. After a moment, they recognized their own street, and then their own house.

"Wow!" said Jay. "How did you do that?"

"I did nothing," said Mr. Jenkins. "Once you knew what to look for, it was easy to find."

Jay and Theresa shrugged, but they watched the pages again. The words began to take shape.

At the top of the page, in bright, gold lettering, the words swirled.

Eventually, the swirling words spelled out, "There's No Place Like Home."

"That's it!" said Jay, pointing at the page.

Theresa narrowed her eyes. "What?" she asked.

"I found a framed needlepoint in the garage," Jay explained. "It said 'There's No Place Like Home,' just like that page!"

Theresa narrowed her eyes at Jay. "You didn't tell me about that," said Theresa.

"I didn't think it mattered at the time," Jay said.

"There is a powerful spell on your house," Mr. Jenkins said, squinting at the book. "According to this book, nearly every house in Ravens Pass has a similar spell on it." He closed the book softly. "That would explain why so few people ever leave this place."

"Thanks, Mr. Jenkins," said Jay. He turned toward Theresa and grabbed her wrist. "Let's get home," he said as he pulled her toward the stairs. "Maybe if we destroy that needlepoint, the spell will be broken."

Theresa nodded. "And the house will have to let us leave," she said.

As Theresa and Jay hurried up the steps, they heard Mr. Jenkins laugh.

"This is Ravens Pass!" he cried out between chuckles. "It's never that easy."

Chapter 7

CAUGHT

Jay and Theresa dropped their bikes in the snow on the front lawn and hurried inside. "Mom?" Jay called out. "Dad?"

There was no response.

"Where could they be?" Theresa asked, running from room to room.

"Maybe they fell asleep," Jay said, jogging upstairs. "They were both exhausted, after all."

But their parents weren't in their room. Jay even checked all the bedroom closets, remembering what had happened to him.

There was no sign of Mom and Dad anywhere in the house.

"Jay!" Theresa called up the steps. "Did you notice anything different down here?"

Jay rushed to the banister. "What?" he asked.

"All the boxes," Theresa said. "They're gone. They must have finished loading the truck."

Jay frowned. "The house probably isn't too happy about that," he said. He hurried downstairs and threw open the door to the garage.

"Empty!" he said as Theresa came up behind him. "That means they already packed the needlepoint."

"Wouldn't that break the spell?" asked Theresa. "I mean, if it's not in the house anymore?"

Jay shrugged. "Let's find out," he said.

Jay hurried to the living room and grabbed a chair. It was as heavy as a boulder. "I guess not," he said.

"We have to find Mom and Dad," Theresa said. "The house might have trapped them someplace. And you saw what that curtain rod tried to do to Dad. They could be hurt."

Jay nodded. Theresa was right. He ran to the basement door.

"It's locked," Jay said. He pounded on the door. "Mom! Dad! Are you down there?" There was no reply.

"They're in trouble, Jay," said Theresa. "We have to break down the door!"

"What if you're wrong?" Jay asked. "If we break the door and they're just fine, they'll ground us for the rest of our lives."

Theresa took his hand. "Come on," she said. "We can peek through the basement windows."

The little windows in the house's old foundation were covered with years of dirt and grime. Theresa and Jay used packed snow to scrub away the muck until there was a clean spot just big enough to peer through.

In the basement, they could see Mom and Dad caught in a wicked tangle of pipes. The metal web wove around their arms and legs. It held their heads in place, and wrapped itself around their ankles like the tentacles of a giant, iron octopus.

Theresa squinted through the thick, old glass. "Why aren't they trying to escape?" she said, her voice shaking.

"I don't think they can," said Jay. "Their eyes are closed. And they're not moving."

Jay and Theresa hurried back to the basement door. "Mom!" Jay said, pounding on the door with his fists. "Dad! Wake up!"

"What if they're —" said Theresa. She couldn't even finish the sentence.

"They're not," said Jay. "The house wants to keep us here. It doesn't want to hurt us."

"Then why won't they wake up?" Theresa said. "How could the house make them sleep like that?"

"I don't know," he said. "And I don't care. We have to get down there to help them."

Jay slammed his shoulder against the basement door. And again. The house moaned each time, but the door didn't budge.

Theresa scrunched up her face. "Do you smell that?" she asked.

Jay sniffed. "Is that . . . ?"

"The gas line!" Theresa said. "That's why they're asleep. The house must've flooded the basement with gas!"

"The cutoff valve is in the basement," Jay said. He thumped against the door again. "It's no use. The door won't budge."

"Great," said Theresa.

"There must be one outside too," said Jay. Again, he slammed against the door. This time he heard something crack.

"I'll go check outside for a cutoff," said Theresa. "You keep trying to break the door down."

Jay nodded. Theresa ran out the back door. The snow in the yard was piled against the house in a big drift, and the wind was picking up.

The cold gusts wrapped around her neck and sent shivers down her spine.

Theresa lowered her head and pushed against the deep snow in the backyard. The bitter winds seemed to be trying to blow her back into the house.

Finally, Theresa reached the gas meter on the back of the garage.

Dials on the meter flipped wildly. It was a confusing mess of cables, skinny pipes, and two big pipes. She ran her fingers over its surface, hoping something would stand out as the cutoff.

Theresa's fingers quickly grew cold, then numb. But she couldn't give up. She had to save Mom and Dad.

Theresa wrapped her shaking fingers around a red handle.

She pulled the handle, but it didn't budge. She tried using both hands. The lever creaked and struggled, like the house was pulling it back the other way.

Her fingers ached. Her wrists protested in pain. But inch by inch, the red lever began to move. It squeaked and vibrated in her hands. The gas meter began to shake and the pipes shook violently. As the lever finally clicked into position, the whole house seemed to let out a loud scream.

Then the squeaking and screaming and shaking all stopped. "I did it!" Theresa cried. She ran over to the basement window and peered through. Inside, bit by bit, her parents slowly opened their eyes.

Chapter 8

IT'S OVER

Jay stood in front of the door with his hands on his knees, catching his breath. The door was beginning to splinter where it met the jamb. One more good thump would probably break the lock, or the hinges. Then the door would open.

Jay's shoulder throbbed in pain. But he had to try one more time.

"Jay!" Theresa said as she ran into the kitchen. "I did it!"

Jay ignored her. It was now or never. He ran at the door, shoulder first. As he did, the door swung open.

Jay nearly tumbled head first down the steps.

"Jay!" shouted Mom. "What are you doing?"

"I was trying to save you!" he said.

"Well, we don't need saving," said Dad. He looked pretty groggy. His clothes were torn and dirty. Mom's hair was a tangled mess.

Mom and Dad slowly walked to the dining room and sat in the chairs — the only place left for all of them to sit in the near-empty house.

"What happened down there?" Jay said. "How did you get trapped?"

Dad shook his head. "When we were finished loading the truck," he said, "I heard what sounded like a dripping pipe downstairs. So we went down to the basement to check it out, and . . ." Dad shrugged.

"Anyway," Mom said, "where have you two been?"

"Anyway," Dad said without waiting for Jay or Theresa to respond. "I heard a dripping pipe, so we went down to the basement to check it out."

"Then we just passed out for some reason," Mom added. "When we woke up, we were lying on the ground in the basement."

"We know why," said Jay. "But to stop it, we need to find something."

"A framed needlepoint," said Theresa. "Jay saw it this morning. It was in the garage."

Mom frowned, then nodded. "Yes, I saw it," she said. "It must have been something Dad's grandmother made."

"That's what I thought —" Jay started to say.

"We can't keep everything, though," Dad said.

"What?" Theresa said. "What do you mean?"

"We threw it out," Mom said.

Jay and Theresa stared at each other, their eyes wide.

"Do you think . . . ?" said Jay.

Theresa shrugged. "I don't know," she said. "Maybe it's enough?"

Mom and Dad stared at them with puzzled looks on their faces.

"Will one of you tell us what's going on?" Dad said.

"Nothing," said Jay. "I think it's over."

"Yeah," Theresa said. "It's totally nothing."

Mom narrowed her eyes at them.

"Okay, then," Mom said, shrugging. "Let's get this dining room set loaded, finally."

It was easy. Sure, it took all of them to move the table, but there was nothing unusual about that. It was a big table, and the remaining three chairs were as heavy as dining room chairs should be.

Before long, everything was in the truck. Dad pulled down the back door and locked it.

"That's the last of it," said Dad. He climbed into the front seat of the rented truck. He turned the key. The big engine coughed and then growled to life. Great puffs of dark, gray smoke spat out from the tailpipe. The air smelled like burning diesel.

"Ready to go!" Dad said with his head out the window. "So, who's coming with me?"

"That thing stinks," said Theresa, pinching her nose. "I'm going with Mom in the car."

Jay shrugged and climbed into the truck.

Before Theresa and Mom were in the family's hatchback, the truck rumbled out of the driveway. The moment all four tires were on the street, the earth began to rumble. The electrical cables — thirty feet off the ground — snapped and popped, sending sparks in every direction.

The street itself shook. A huge crack grew out of the house and crawled along the ground until it reached the asphalt of the street. Cracks radiated outward in every direction from the curb, sending big chunks of pavement flying into the air.

"It's not over!" Jay shouted out the truck's open window. "Quick, Theresa! Get Mom in the car and get out of here."

Jay turned to his father in the driver's seat. "Go, Dad!" he shouted. "We have to get out of here!"

Dad shifted the truck into gear and slammed on the gas pedal. The truck grunted and struggled against the crumbling, icy roads. Finally, the tires got a grip and the truck jolted forward. As it did, the street quaked terribly.

Then the pavement rose up in front of them like a huge tidal wave.

Watching from the driveway, Theresa slammed her car door closed. She shouted at her mom, "Get in! We have to get out of here. The house is possessed!"

"What?" Mom cried out. She climbed into the car and started it up. As she pulled away, they saw the moving truck tumble over and land on its side with a violent screech of metal on pavement. Its back door flung open, sending all their possessions across the snow-covered lawn.

Mom veered to avoid crashing into the truck. But she steered straight onto the grass and crashed into the fire hydrant. The car was totaled, and the hydrant spewed out water like a geyser.

Theresa climbed out of the car and shouted into the wind for her brother and father.

The two of them climbed out of the truck and stumbled toward Theresa and Mom. "We're all okay," Mom said, hugging her family.

Dad nodded. "But we're not going anywhere now," he said. The family stood together and looked at the house. A fire had started in the line of pine trees next to the house. Their dry needles acted like kindling, and the broken electric cables like a lighter.

Soon the sirens of the Ravens Pass fire department screamed in the distance.

Chapter 9

STAYING

Before long, the Mills family was drinking cups of hot cider.

The whole block had come out to see what was happening. Neighbors stood on their front lawns and watched.

The fire department, the water department, and the electric company had all come too.

Dad had a wool blanket wrapped around his shoulders as he looked through the stuff spread all over the lawn. "Most of our stuff seems fine," he said.

The fire chief, his face black with soot, walked up to them. He put a hand on Dad's shoulder. "You've been very lucky," he said. "There was almost no damage to the property. A couple of burned trees. The paint on the east side of the house is black, but it'll wash off, I'd bet."

"Thank goodness," Mom said. "We still haven't sold the house. It would be hard to sell it with much damage."

"Sell the house?" the fire chief repeated. He pushed back his helmet. "You mean that moving truck is yours? All this stuff is yours?"

Dad nodded.

The fire chief laughed a little. "Don't you people know?" he spoke in a rough whisper. "No one leaves Ravens Pass." He shook his head and then walked away.

ABOUT THE AUTHOR

STEVE BREZENOFF lives in Minneapolis, Minnesota, with his wife, Beth, and their son, Sam. Besides writing books, he enjoys playing video games, riding his bicycle, and helping middle-school students to improve their writing skills. Steve's ideas almost always come to him in his dreams, so he does his best writing in his pajamas.

ABOUT THE ILLUSTRATOR

A long time ago, when AMERIGO PINELLI was very small, his mother gave him a pencil. From that moment on, drawing became his world. Nowadays, Amerigo works as an illustrator above the narrow streets and churches of Naples, Italy. He loves his job because it feels more like play than work. And each morning, as the sun rises over Mount Vesuvius, Amerigo gets to chase pigeons along the rooftops. Just ask his lovely wife, Giulia, if you don't believe him.

GLOSSARY

BANISTER (BAN-iss-tur)—a railing that runs along the side of a flight of stairs

BIRD OF PREY (BIRD UV PRAY)—a bird that hunts and kills other animals, like a hawk or an owl

BUREAU (BYUR-oh)—a chest of drawers

DESERTED (di-ZURT-id)—left behind or abandoned

HAVEN (HAY-vuhn)—a safe place

MISCHIEVOUS (MISS-chuh-vuhss)—playful and annoying behavior that may cause harm to others

NEEDLEPOINT (NEE-duhl-poynt)—embroidery on canvas, usually with a stitching pattern

PLASTER (PLASS-tur)—a substance made of lime, sand, and water, used by builders on walls or ceilings

UNDERSTATEMENT (UHN-dur-state-ment)—the act of stating something in restrained terms, or as less than it actually is

DISCUSSION QUESTIONS

1. Jay and Theresa have to save their parents all by themselves. Have you ever had to help someone who is older than you? Talk about times you've helped an adult.

2. Ravens Pass is a town where crazy things happen. Has anything spooky or creepy ever happened where you live? Talk about scary or strange stories you've heard.

3. Do you believe in poltergeists, or evil ghosts that can possess physical objects? Why or why not?

WRITING PROMPTS

1. What happens after the Mills family decides to stay in Ravens Pass? Write another chapter to this book.

2. Write a short story about a house that is possessed and trying to scare away its owners. How does it try to scare the residents away?

3. Write a newspaper article describing what occurs in this book. What do the Mills have to say about the recent events?

POLTERGEIST OR PRANK?

Two nights ago, the Mills family called the police. They filed a report stating that their house was possessed by evil spirts. Police investigated the home and found plenty of structural damage — but the police claim the damage was caused by the Mills family, not a ghost or evil spirit.

But when I interviewed the Mills family and took a tour of their house, I found out much more information. So much, in fact, that I don't quite know what to believe anymore . . .

I saw pipes in the basement which were bent to such a degree that I find it hard to believe human hands could have done it. I saw a fissure in the earth that could not possibly be human-made. The fissure passed right beneath the Mills' home, no less!

BELIEVE US, THERE'S A LOT OF IT!

EYE

So, readers, what do you think really happened? I'll tell you what the police want us to think: the Mills family did it. But I know that you know better, reader. For one thing, why would the Mills family destroy their own house? What purpose would that serve?

And this is Ravens Pass we're talking about. Strange things happen here every day. The answer is clear: we have a haunted house in Ravens Pass.

Man-made disaster, or poltergeist?

MORE
DARK TALES

FROM
RAVENS PASS

RAVENS PASS

LOOKING
FOR ALL TYPES OF
CREEPY CRAWLY
SPOOKY
GHOULISH TALES?

CHECK OUT
WWW.CAPSTONEKIDS.COM
FOR MORE
SCARY BOOKS!

Find cool websites and more books
like this one at www.facthound.com.

Just type in the Book ID:
9781434246158